THEA'S TREE

ALISON JACKSON

~ *Illustrated by* ~

JANET PEDERSEN

~ DUTTON CHILDREN'S BOOKS ~

This one is for all my friends
at the Seminole County Public Library!
—A.J.

For Ruthie
—J.P.

DUTTON CHILDREN'S BOOKS   A division of Penguin Young Readers Group

Published by the Penguin Group • Penguin Group (USA) Inc., 375 Hudson Street, New York, New York 10014, U.S.A.
Penguin Group (Canada), 90 Eglinton Avenue East, Suite 700, Toronto, Ontario, Canada M4P 2Y3 (a division of Pearson Penguin
Canada Inc.) • Penguin Books Ltd, 80 Strand, London WC2R 0RL, England • Penguin Ireland, 25 St Stephen's Green, Dublin 2, Ireland
(a division of Penguin Books Ltd) • Penguin Group (Australia), 250 Camberwell Road, Camberwell, Victoria 3124, Australia (a division
of Pearson Australia Group Pty Ltd) • Penguin Books India Pvt Ltd, 11 Community Centre, Panchsheel Park, New Delhi – 110 017, India •
Penguin Group (NZ), 67 Apollo Drive, Rosedale, North Shore 0632, New Zealand (a division of Pearson New Zealand Ltd) •
Penguin Books (South Africa) (Pty) Ltd, 24 Sturdee Avenue, Rosebank, Johannesburg 2196, South Africa

Penguin Books Ltd, Registered Offices: 80 Strand, London WC2R 0RL, England

Text copyright © 2008 by Alison Jackson
Illustrations copyright © 2008 by Janet Pedersen

Library of Congress Cataloging-in-Publication Data

Jackson, Alison, date.
Thea's tree / by Alison Jackson; illustrated by Janet Pedersen.
      p. cm.
Summary: Thea Teawinkle plants an odd, purple, bean-shaped seed in her front yard for her class science project, with astonishing
results that even the experts she writes to—including a botanist, an arborist, a museum curator, and a symphony director—cannot
offer any explanations for.

ISBN: 978-0-525-47443-2 (hardcover)
[1. Science projects—Fiction. 2. Plants—Fiction. 3. Letters—Fiction. 4. Humorous stories.] I. Pedersen, Janet, ill. II. Title.

PZ7.J13217Th 2008   [E]—dc22 2007005220

Published in the United States
by Dutton Children's Books,
a division of Penguin Young Readers Group
345 Hudson Street, New York, New York 10014
www.penguin.com/youngreaders

Designed by Irene Vandervoort

Manufactured in China
First Edition
10 9 8 7 6 5 4 3 2 1

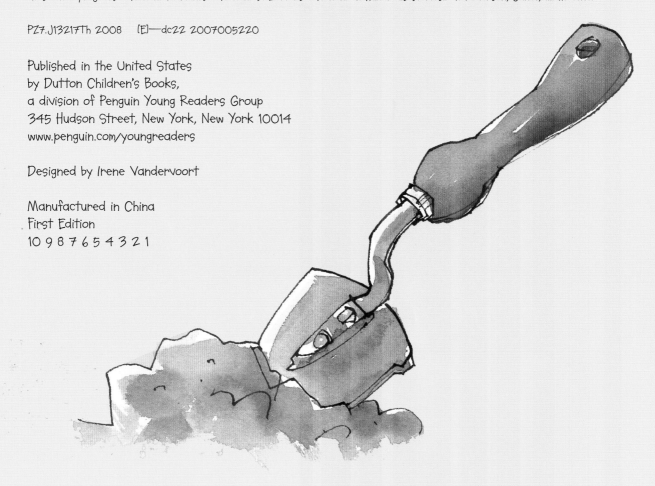

One Monday morning, the students in Ms. Rankin's science class found a message on the chalkboard in Room #3A.

FUTURE SCIENTIST PROJECT

Pick a subject of scientific interest to you.

Do research on your topic.

Observe, and keep track of your findings.

Include them in a report.

And have fun!

Your project is due in one month.

FUTURE SCIENTIST PROJECT

Presented to: Ms. Rankin, Room #3A
Sunny Valley Elementary School

Three days ago I planted a seed in my front yard.
It was a purple seed, shaped a little like a peanut, only
not as big. The seed hasn't sprouted yet, but the dirt
all around it is turning purple, and the ground looks sort of
oozy and bubbly. Mommy says she's never seen anything like
it in Topeka, Kansas. So I am going to watch the seed for
a month to see what happens. What do you think?

Curiously,
Thea Teawinkle,
Future Scientist

DRAWING OF PURPLE SEED

Mr. Bertram Beaman, Botanist
Topeka Horticultural Society
Topeka, Kansas

Dear Mr. Beaman:

Six days ago I planted a seed in the front yard. The dirt around it turned all purple and bubbly, and now my seed has sprouted giant purple leaves that are very strong and nearly an inch and a half thick! I think my plant might be some kind of purple African rubber plant. Is this possible?

Excitedly,
Thea Teawinkle

Ms. Thea Teawinkle
222 Tuttle Creek Turnpike
Topeka, Kansas

Dear Ms. Teawinkle:

Unfortunately, there are no purple African rubber plants growing in Topeka, Kansas. The seed in question does sound quite fascinating, but your hardy plant is probably a strong breed of common prairie orchid. Could you perhaps send a photograph?

Helpfully,
Bertram Beaman
Botanist

Ms. Anna Applebaum, Arboreal Acquisitions
Topeka Arboretum
Topeka, Kansas

Dear Ms. Applebaum:

Nine days ago I planted a seed in the front yard. At first I thought it was a purple African rubber plant, but Mr. Beaman at the Horticultural Society told me there are no purple African rubber plants growing in Topeka, Kansas. My plant is now a big tree with a trunk that is ten feet around—with vines and branches large enough to hold a grown man!

Could I have possibly planted a giant Venus flytrap?

Anxiously,
Thea Teawinkle

Ms. Thea Teawinkle
222 Tuttle Creek Turnpike
Topeka, Kansas

Dear Ms. Teawinkle:

I'm sorry to disappoint you, dear. But your suggestion is impossible. Simply impossible. There are *no* giant Venus flytraps growing in Topeka, Kansas, that look like that. Undoubtedly, your plant is some form of purple elder or cottonwood tree, native to this area.

Importantly,
Anna Applebaum
Arboreal Acquisitions

WILLIAM FIR

FLUFFY ELDER

Mr. Carl Capshaw, Curator
Natural History Museum
Topeka, Kansas

Dear Mr. Capshaw:

Twelve days ago I planted a seed in the front yard.
At first I thought it was a purple African rubber plant
or a giant Venus flytrap. But there are no purple African
rubber plants or giant Venus flytraps in Topeka, Kansas.
Besides, my tree has now shot up beyond the roof of our
house—in less than two weeks! I can hardly see the top
of it.

Could my tree actually be a giant redwood?

Eagerly,
Thea Teawinkle

Ms. Thea Teawinkle
222 Tuttle Creek Turnpike
Topeka, Kansas

Dear Ms. Teawinkle:

Wow! I've never seen a giant redwood within a hundred miles of Topeka, Kansas! But I'd sure love to have one for my museum. Your plant sounds more like a common red cedar than a giant redwood anyway, but I have never heard of cedars that mature so rapidly. (How often do you water yours?)

Enthusiastically,

Carl Capshaw
Curator

WILDLIFE OF THE ANDES

FUTURE SITE OF THEA'S TREE

Ms. Zoe Zimmerman, Zoologist
Topeka Zoo
Topeka, Kansas

Dear Ms. Zimmerman:

Two weeks ago I planted a seed in my front yard. It has since sprouted into a gigantic tree that is not a rubber plant or a Venus flytrap or a giant redwood, because I have been told there are no purple rubber plants or Venus flytraps or giant redwoods in Topeka, Kansas. But whatever it is, something very large has decided to build a nest in it.

I know this for a fact, because yesterday I found an egg lying on the ground, right next to the tree's trunk. The weird thing is that the egg didn't break from the fall. It never even cracked! What's weirder is that the egg is very large, and appears to be made completely of gold. Besides that, I can hear strange rumbling and growling noises coming from somewhere up in the branches.

Do you think there is a giant ostrich living in my tree?

Hopefully,
Thea Teawinkle

Ms. Thea Teawinkle
222 Tuttle Creek Turnpike
Topeka, Kansas

Dear Ms. Teawinkle:

a. There are no ostriches roaming wild in Topeka, Kansas.

b. There are, however, plenty of wild prairie chickens here.

c. Prairie chicken eggs are often quite large and brownish-
gold in color.

d. Admittedly, an egg like the one you describe is rare
indeed—especially in Topeka. But the fact remains:
That egg came from a chicken!

Alphabetically,
Zoe Zimmerman
Zoologist

P.S. If you ever get hold of the chicken that laid that egg,
I'd love to have a look at it.

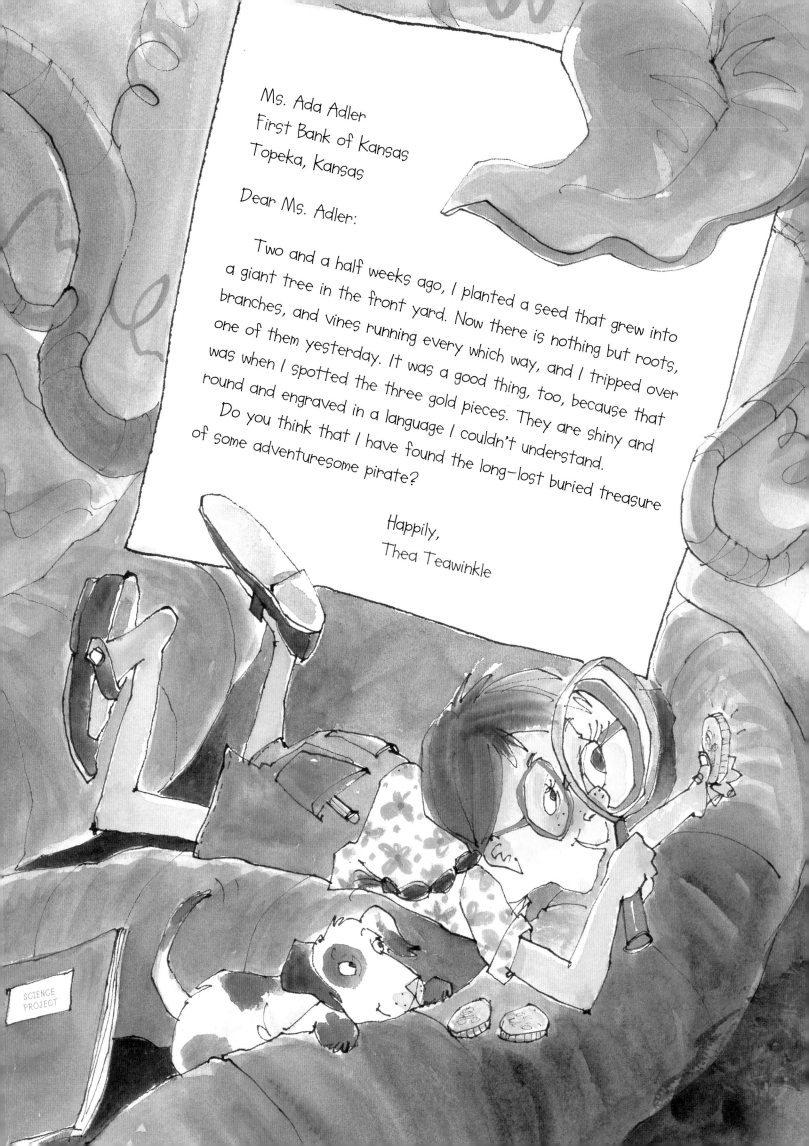

Ms. Ada Adler
First Bank of Kansas
Topeka, Kansas

Dear Ms. Adler:

Two and a half weeks ago, I planted a seed that grew into a giant tree in the front yard. Now there is nothing but roots, branches, and vines running every which way, and I tripped over one of them yesterday. It was a good thing, too, because that was when I spotted the three gold pieces. They are shiny and round and engraved in a language I couldn't understand. Do you think that I have found the long-lost buried treasure of some adventuresome pirate?

Happily,
Thea Teawinkle

SCIENCE
PROJECT

Ms. Thea Teawinkle
222 Tuttle Creek Turnpike
Topeka, Kansas

Dear Ms. Teawinkle:

There were never any pirates in Topeka, Kansas. And if there were, they would have been far more "lost" than your buried treasure. Take another look, and you'll see that your coins are most likely common artifacts from one of the early Native American tribes inhabiting this area.

Doubtfully,
Ada Adler
First Bank of Kansas

Mr. Derek Dreyer, Director
Topeka Philharmonic Orchestra
Topeka, Kansas

Dear Mr. Dreyer:

Three weeks ago I planted a seed in the front yard (what's left of the front yard, that is). The seed grew into a giant tree that is now so thick and so tall that the sun never shines in our yard anymore. In fact, it was so dark out there yesterday that I would never have found the harp at all if it hadn't been for the singing. That's right. I found a singing harp...just lying there among the roots of the giant tree trunk with the vines on it.

Is your orchestra missing a harp by any chance? And if it is, do you know how the singing harp ended up under my tree?

Confusedly,
Thea Teawinkle

Ms. Thea Teawinkle
222 Tuttle Creek Turnpike
Topeka, Kansas

Dear Ms. Teawinkle:
I am a busy man, and I have no time for practical jokes. If you did indeed find such an object as you describe, it is obviously some sort of outdated musical instrument, no doubt left over from the steamboat days on the Missouri River. Perhaps it has been buried all these years, only to be unearthed by the roots of your enormous tree. Be that as it may, I hardly think such an instrument would produce music at all after 130 years, let alone sing!

Industriously,
Derek Dreyer
Director

Mr. Thomas Trent
Trent Tree Removal
Topeka, Kansas

Dear Mr. Trent:

Four weeks ago I planted a seed that grew into a giant tree in the front yard. The tree is so big now that our family hasn't seen the sun in nearly a month! Roots and vines are creeping up through the bathroom pipes, and branches block all of the windows. Yesterday we finally lost all radio and telephone communication. My parents are really upset with me, but they can't send me to my room, because it looks like a Brazilian rain forest. And they can't cut the thing down either, because the garage (and all of Dad's tools) are buried, too. Can you please come and remove my tree? Soon?

Desperately,
Thea Teawinkle

To: Ms. Rankin, Room #3A
Sunny Valley Elementary School
Topeka, Kansas

Dear Ms. Rankin:
    I'm sorry to report that I still cannot identify the plant in my yard. Six experts have not been able to answer any of my questions, and now Mr. Trent of Trent Tree Removal says he can't even cut the thing down!
    There's nothing left to do, but

Two days later, the students in Ms. Rankin's science class handed in their Future Scientist Projects.

FINAL REPORT

Presented by Thea Teawinkle

One month ago I planted a seed in my front yard. As the seed grew into a tree, I questioned some specialists and kept track of my findings. I won't be needing their advice any longer. Everyone told me there was no tree like mine in Topeka, Kansas, and I guess they were right. As I was writing this final report I heard a crash, and when I went outside to see what happened, the tree had completely disappeared. I searched the entire yard, and nothing was there. Even the egg, the coins, and the singing harp were gone! I did find some really large footprints, though.

I'm going to write a letter to Mr. Shakley of Shakley's Shoe Mart to see if he is missing any shoes that are size 112. Maybe this could be the start of a whole new project!